Stranded with the
– A Short, Steamy Insta... ... ...ountain Man
Romance

Mountain Men of Charming Falls

By Ann Ric

Books by Ann Ric

Mountain Men of Charming Falls

Rescued by the Mountain Man (Evie & Jake)
Claimed by the Mountain Man (Candi & Erik)
Stranded with the Mountain Man (Lilly & Alex)
Christmas with the Mountain Man (Harmony & Chase)

Magic Protector Reverse Harem Trilogy

Magic Protector – A Steamy Paranormal Reverse Harem Romance (Book 1)
Magic Bound – A Steamy Paranormal Reverse Harem Romance (Book 2)
Magic Promise – A Steamy Paranormal Reverse Harem Romance (Book 3)

Stranded with the Mountain Man

After her boss, who is also her ex, leaves her at the company's camping trip site, Lilly finds herself stranded in the middle of a brewing storm...

Until she's rescued by a gorgeous, grumpy ex-military mountain man with the most breathtaking physique and stunning features she's ever seen. She's supposed to be on a break from dating, so why is she falling for this hero?

***

Welcome to ***Mountain Men of Charming Falls***, the spicy instalove series based on a picturesque small mountain town by a lake that brings you closer to nature. A tranquil scenic escape from the busy city where residents in the cozy close-knit community look out for each other. Let the cool mountain breeze, clear night skies, beautiful romantic sunsets, and the fresh pine scents that fill the air bring you serene relaxation. Known for its camping sites, rustic cabin retreats, hiking trails, ski slopes, and yes, semi-recluse hot and sexy ex-military mountain men who live by the honor code: respect, loyalty, selfless service, integrity and courage in everything they do. Charming Falls is the perfect place to fall in love.

Chapter 1 - Lilly

"Oh, no. This is so not happening," Lilly said, mostly to herself, as she wondered through the wooded area of Charming Falls, glancing nervously over her shoulder every time she heard a crack in the fallen tree branches, wondering if an animal was nearby.

She was lost.

Lost in the woods, of all places.

She knew it wasn't safe to stay in a cold car but walking outside couldn't be any better. She trudged through the snow with her boots, feeling soaked inside, as she searched for a cabin or a store where she could get warm and call for help. Her car battery had died. Both she and her car needed a boost right now.

She was cold and hungry and furious right now.

Jack had set her up. He'd set her up at the company and now she was out of a job in the middle of a company trip to the mountains. And she was freezing.

The job paid well and in fact, it was helping to cover her brother Samuel's physical therapy treatments. The medical insurance alone was worth the job. Her brother needed physical therapy three times a week for his cerebral palsy. He meant the world to Lilly. That was the only reason she hadn't told Jack to take the job and shove it where the sun didn't shine.

Their mother was a single mom working in a dead-end job and couldn't afford it—and their dad wasn't in the picture.

Lilly had put up with her boss Jack's antics so that she could continue to cover her brother's medical care. But she had other prospects on the horizon. She was looking at opening up her own little ad agency where she could take on one or two clients since she'd been coming up with all the creative ideas at her ex's agency and not getting the credit for it. She should just venture out on her own. It had been her dream. The new client prospect, a mountain retreat company, had even liked her ideas and wanted to work directly with her.

Oh, well. That wasn't going to happen now. It won't be easy but she would have to find a way. She wasn't going to give up that easily.

How did she get herself into this situation?

The storm clouds above didn't offer any kind of reassurance right now. If she didn't find shelter soon, she'd be in deep trouble.

She glanced down at her phone to see one bar on her WIFI.

How could Jack do this to her?

How on earth was she to know that he would be the boss at her department at the agency? Of all places.

Two years!

It had been two years since she broke off with Jack after he'd cheated on her. And the guy still had it in for her.

It was as if she just couldn't get that guy out of her life.

Well, he was out of her life now. At the worst possible time.

Her friend, Daphne, said her cousin Alexander lived on the mountains. She wondered if she could find his cabin and ask to borrow his phone. She'd met him a few times. Her heart fluttered in her chest thinking of him. He was strikingly good-looking. And he was also nice to her. A little distant but they hadn't spent much time together.

Lilly glanced at her phone screen again and then dialed Daphne's number. Yep, she never liked to use speed dial or programmed numbers. Her mother always told her it was important to always have numbers in your head that you could call by mechanical memory just in case you didn't have your phone with you or your phone died and you had to use someone else's to call your closest friends or family members.

"Hey, girl. Why do you sound so out of breath?" Daphne answered over the phone.

The call was chipping out so Lilly only caught a few words.

"I'm not out of breath, I'm lost in the woods, talking and walking, trying to find my way out of here."

"What? Why? What happened? Aren't you with your coworkers?"

"Nope. Not anymore."

This was supposed to be the company's annual camping trip and retreat on the mountains of Charming Falls. A weekend for the employees to clear their minds and spark their creativity in the wilderness as they tried to clinch the deal on a potential new client project.

Daphne knew the whole story. How Lilly worked at that advertising company as a junior and hoped to work her way up. Things were going great…until her ex showed up in her department—as the new boss. He'd stolen most of her ideas and passed them off as his own.

Then…he made Lilly's life hell, to put it mildly. The work environment had become toxic to say the least. But this was the last straw.

"What do you mean, not anymore?" Daphne queried.

"I quit."

"You quit? Just like that?"

"Not exactly. He was giving me a hard time. He kept sabotaging my work and purposely leaving me out of company meetings. Then, we were supposed to meet a new client up here—a mountain retreat company."

"And?"

"He told me I left the files behind but I didn't."

"You had them with you?"

"No. You see, he didn't tell me to bring the artwork. He was just making it up."

"He can't do that."

"He can and he did. Then he told me I was fired."

"He fired you?"

"Well, I told him I quit. I wouldn't want that to be on my record. I wouldn't be surprised if he moved to my department just to make my life hell."

"You can't let him get away with that."

"I won't. I'll fight it in court, but for now…I need to get out of the woods. My car died."

"Oh, no."

Lilly should never have gone out with Jack in the first place. What did she ever see in him. She had broken up with him after she caught him cheating with a super thin model. A woman who was totally the opposite of Lilly. Lilly had curves—too many for his liking. There was never a day that he didn't make her aware of that. He'd always drop hints about her losing weight or exercising more. Whenever they were out, his head would always turn in the direction of a skinny girl walking past them. Then…she caught him with one of her neighbors on her block. She'd had enough. The reason why he wanted to stay together with her was had nothing to do with love. And she knew that now. He was sore she broke up with him. His ego was bruised. So now, he was getting his revenge. But he won't win.

"Girl, you need to get inside where it's nice and warm. You know my cousin Alexander, right?"

Oh, she remembered him all right. The tall, dark and sinfully handsome, heavily tattooed ex-military soldier. He rarely spoke to anyone but he was always so supportive of Daphne and the family. He was hot. She'd caught him glancing at her at that fundraising barbecue Daphne and she held one day.

"He lives around Cedar Lane, right?"

"Yeah. It's actually *off* Cedar Lane. It's on a long dirt road called Second Chance Lane. I have no idea why it's called that. He and some of his army buddies have decided to live the life of a recluse on the mountain. So many people moving into cabins up there. Anyway, you should…"

The phone went dead.

"Daphne!" Lilly said, panic in her voice.

The sound of silence filled the air as Lilly stared in horror at her phone screen as she continued to walk, the sound of her footsteps crunching on the gravel road. Her phone call dropped and seconds later, so did her body.

"Ouch."

Lilly stumbled and tripped over a large fallen tree branch that had been partly covered by snow.

"Oh, great. This is just what I need. To be lost in the woods and immobile," she murmured under her breath as pain coursed through her ankle.

"Could this day get any worse?" she groaned.

When she heard the sound of a low growl coming from an animal behind her, she realized the answer to that question was a resounding yes.

Chapter 2 - Alex

Alex finished chopping wood for his neighbor, Mrs. K, for her fireplace.

Mrs. K had moved to a cabin in the mountains with her husband, a war hero, who'd built the cabin for them to live the rest of their lives in. It wasn't a typical retirement home since most seniors liked to live in warmer climates but the Ks loved it. Sadly, her husband of 40 years passed away and now she lived there alone. She'd told him she wanted to stay in the cabin where they were both happy.

He liked that about her. He didn't believe in this happily ever after thing she always spoke about, but he was happy for her. And protective too.

As an ex-military soldier himself, Alex liked to look out for fellow vets. It was an honor to be there for them, especially the older ones who'd served in one of the deadliest wars in recent history.

Alex made sure to take care of Mrs. K and made sure she was all right, especially since her own grown children didn't visit often.

He wiped a sweat off his brow.

There was a storm brewing in the mountains, so everyone had to make sure they had everything they needed to wait it out, including a warm cabin. The temperatures were below freezing at this time of the year.

"You are such a dear," Mrs. K said after Alex finished placing the wood in the fireplace. He also placed some extra wood down by the side.

"No problem, Mrs. K. That should be enough for now," he said. He wasn't very good with communicating and socializing with people. That's why he liked living on the mountains. Away from most people. Except when he went to the Charming Falls Cozy Bar & Grill in the town and met up with his army buddies for a drink. Many of them lived around the area too in their own cabins.

Alex mostly kept to himself after he'd come back from serving overseas. Everything had changed for him. He was no longer the same person.

"I know you'll find the right woman one day," she blurted out.

She knew, didn't she? Mrs. K. knew about Alex's heartbreak and how he came to the mountains to get away from it all.

"Thanks, but I'm not really looking right now," he said, sincerely.

"Oh, come now. You're like a son to me. I want to see you happy. You're a good man. You didn't deserve that woman messing around behind your back."

Great. He guessed *that* story got around. Thanks to social media. Something he never really understood.

"Is there anything else I can do for you, Mrs. K?" he asked, wanting to make sure she was okay.

"I think I have everything I need, dear. You already brought my groceries and stocked up my fridge. Thank you so much."

"No problem. Just give me a call if you need anything at all. I'll come back and check on you later."

"I have my phone right here beside me. Thank you for charging it. You take care too. Don't stay out too long."

"I won't."

He smiled as he left her cabin. He really appreciated Mrs. K.

She and her husband were like second parents to him. He'd do anything for her and to make sure she was safe, especially now that her husband was gone.

It was a good thing her cabin wasn't far from his. He looked up at the grey clouds and felt the heavy winds circling around him. The chill in the air was harsh. No one should be out there right now. It got pretty bad, especially out there on the mountains.

The snow was going to come down heavy soon.

After he got into his pick-up truck, he made his way down the winding road. It wasn't long before he saw something in the woods. Against the blanket of white snow, he saw a woman in a red coat. Her hair swaying in the wind.

Oh, no.

She was a few feet away from a wolf, holding up her handbag as if to shield herself.

He spun his truck around to the direction.

He got out of his vehicle and made a loud noise and frightened the wolf away. It scattered away through the woods.

"Are you all right, ma'am?" he asked, concerned as he walked closer to her.

The woman breathed a sigh of relief and turned around to face him.

His heart almost stopped in his chest.

Man, she was stunning, beautiful. She wore a snug-fit crimson winter jacket that hugged her sensuous curves. She was shaped like an earth angel.

She also looked familiar.

Wasn't she a friend of his cousin? He thought he'd seen her somewhere before on his cousin's Facebook page. Not that he was on social media these days. They were doing some sort of fundraiser for the kid's hospital and he had gone to the page to make a donation.

He also met her briefly at a community event. He didn't always remember faces, but this angelic face was hard to forget. She was someone he took a liking to when he'd first seen her in the past.

He wanted to ask her but his tongue was tied at the moment. He just wanted to make sure she was safe and unharmed.

His body responded to this lovely curvy woman. His cock moved inside his pants. She was breathtaking. He tried to shift his focus. There was an instant attraction but right now, it looked as if his heart was something he needed to keep guarded.

Chapter 3 - Lilly

"Oh, my God! You saved my life! Thank you!" Lilly said, almost breathless. She sat on a stump to steady herself. Her heartbeat still raced after that near-attack. "I don't know how to thank you enough," she said.

Her eyes drank in the beauty of the handsome stranger before her until recognition swept over her.

Her heart went kaboom in her chest and did that funny fluttering thing. Butterflies sprang inside her belly.

Alexander.

It was Alexander.

And he looked even more stunning than she'd remembered.

Oh, great. How embarrassing that he should see her like this. Literally flat on her face.

He was stunning. His blue eyes were mesmerizing, captivating.

"Alexander," she said.

"My friends call me Alex." He looked sheepish.

"That's right, Alex. I…you probably don't remember me but…"

"Actually, I do now that I see your face."

Their eyes locked for a moment as a warm feeling lingered in the air between them.

"Thanks again. You came at the perfect time," she said, softly, trying to hide her nervousness.

"Hey, it's no trouble. Are you hurt?" he asked, his tone carried an air of concern. His voice was deep and sexy. He stood tall and towered over her as he got near to her. He must be a whole foot taller than her. She was five feet three inches. She was willing to bet he was about six feet three inches tall.

And so tantalizingly gorgeous. He filled out nicely in his winter jacket with his broad shoulders. The space between her legs throbbed with arousal. His jacket was slightly open at the top. She could see he had inked designs on his neck and remembered how incredible his body looked in the summertime. There was something sexy about a muscular guy with tattoos.

She also noticed Alex was extremely polite. Most men who'd served in the army were, she'd noticed. But Alex was the most stunning ex-soldier she'd ever seen.

"I'm fine, thanks. I tripped over a fallen branch but I'm good."

"You sure? You want me to look at your leg for you?"

Her inner thighs pulsed again with pleasure. What was with her? Why on earth did she react to him like that? He only wanted to look at her leg, not anything else.

She didn't know why but an image of him kissing her leg swept into her mind but she sucked in a deep breath and switched her focus. Maybe the cold was getting to her brain.

"Thanks. I don't think I sprained anything though. I was just looking for a phone."

"You lost your phone?" he asked, puzzled.

"No, I actually lost my phone *service*," she emphasized, not understanding why she felt so tongue tied. It was as if she had brain freeze out there in the cold.

As if he read her mind, he asked. "Would you like to come in from the cold?" He thought for a minute. "I live around here." He held out his hand to help her up.

She held his hand while he pulled her up with ease. Man, he was strong. She felt his energy. His hand was firm and strong and she felt tingles erupt down her spine. She didn't always feel this way around a guy. What was with her today? Maybe it had been too long since she last had a date. Like over two years! Still, she'd never met a man like this before who was breathtaking and captivating. The man stopped and came over to help her before he even knew who she was. These days, you don't often find anyone stopping to help a stranger in need. Of course, there were so many scams going around these days that some people were afraid of stopping to help. Not that she was up to anything sinister.

She had just been, after all, in front of a mountain wolf earlier! It wasn't as if they were in cahoots or anything.

Lilly even liked the sound of his name. Alex. Short for Alexander which mean protector or something like that. How fitting.

"You look so different from the last time I saw you," she said, and almost regretted saying that.

The difference was he looked *clothed*, she thought to herself with a grin. The last time she'd seen him, it was a hot day in the town and he was shirtless. Man, his abs were chiseled and looked firm. His breathtaking tats adorned his body like decoration. He never smiled much and he kept his distance. He barely said a few words to her back then.

She remembered how her body felt when she'd first met him last year. And now? Even hotter, especially considering they were in sub-zero temperature.

From the time she first met him, he seemed like a man with a lot on his mind. There was something mysterious about him, in a sweet way. She'd always been intrigued by her friend's cousin.

"How did you end up out here like this?" he asked her later, when he helped her up into his truck. It was a spacious vehicle and he kept it clean. She noticed he had a lot of construction stuff in the back, but it wasn't dirty.

She caught the sweet scent of his cologne and it drove her senses wild.

Now that she was finally near him after all this time since she last saw him, butterflies were flickering in her tummy.

He always made her feel that way. She never thought she'd see him again though she'd always hoped she would. And now her dream had come true and she didn't know what to do about it.

"I was fired," she blurted out.

"Fired?" He arched a sexy brow.

"Well, actually I quit," she clarified. "It's a long story. My company was here on a trip in the woods to meet a potential client who is looking for creating a new ad campaign for their mountain retreat."

"I see," he said, thoughtfully as he drove on the snow-filled road towards his cabin.

"So they left you out in the cold?" He clenched his jaw.

She saw the look of fury in his gorgeous eyes framed by long lashes.

He was furious on her behalf. She didn't know what to think. It was as if they'd known each other for a long time and he was suddenly protective over her. That was so sweet. Daphne had said that her cousin was a protective man when it came to women.

"I drove off but I hadn't realized my tank was low." If she didn't know better she wouldn't put it past Jack to drain her gas tank when she wasn't around. But she didn't want Alex to think she was paranoid or ruin the mood in his nice vehicle.

One moment at a time, Lilly. Take a deep breath and relax.

She was grateful to be alive and in the safe care of this gorgeous mountain man.

Her stomach growled loudly.

"I can get you something to eat. When was the last time you ate?" She adored the deep, rich yet caring tone in his voice.

She was starving but didn't want him to know when she first saw him. But it looked as if her stomach made that announcement for her.

"I'll be fine."

"Hey, I'm not telling you what to do but it's no trouble for me to whip something up quickly. Food is important." He arched a brow. She admired his take-charge personality.

"Well, I guess eating food is better than *being* food," she chuckled.

"I think it's admirable that you have a sense of humor about it all. But that was dangerous," he said, softly. An air of concern in his voice. "You could have been hurt out there." His brows furrowed. "I can't believe they left you out here without any help or made sure you got out of the mountains safely." His lips curled with disgust.

She *could* believe it. Jack was just that type of person. He was nothing like Alex.

"So where did you leave your car, Lilly?" he asked, his voice softened. "I'll give you a boost later. Right now, we're expecting a whiteout any minute."

She loved the way he said her name. Waves of delight filled her. He'd already given her a boost without even realizing it.

There was something sweet and sexy about his energy, his spirit. His eyes were kind and sincere as if she could see the window into his soul. She never felt this way about Jack, ever! Jack was always uptight and angry and very unkind to strangers. What had she ever seen in her ex? It was a good thing she'd found out that he was a cheat before it was too late.

"My car is somewhere around here. I walked a good distance before I met that big bad wolf on the way to grandma's house," she said, jokingly, making a reference to the story of Little Red Riding Hood. The irony was not lost on her that she was actually wearing a red coat too.

He grinned slightly. "Well, I'm glad I got there before the wolf got any closer to you."

"I'm glad you did too. Talk about timing." Talk about kismet, she wanted to add but she didn't.

She'd been so attracted to him when she first met him at that barbecue, when she was single at the time, but she didn't know if she'd ever see him again. She didn't want to mention anything to her friend, Daphne, at the time seeing as how awkward it would have been.

Daphne had told her that another friend of hers dated her other cousin and things got awkward when they broke up. Daphne had to pick sides and she didn't feel good about it afterwards. In fact, Daphne had told Lilly that she ended up not talking to her friend after that.

She'd hate to lose a friend if things got crazy. Why was her mind running away to that scenario? It wasn't as if anything was ever going to happen between she and Alex. He'd just saved her life and wanted to make sure she was safe.

And she'd be alone soon. In his cabin in the mountains. At least until her car got a boost.

"I'll get you inside where you'll be nice and warm first, then I'll go out and look for your car later. The visibility is crazy right now. I might have to get it towed to the garage later."

"Sounds good to me," she said, looking out of the windshield. The weather conditions worsened each minute. How would she have survived out there if Alex hadn't seen her in time? If the wolf didn't get to her, the storm might have. Yikes.

"Thank you for doing that for me," she said again. She couldn't wait to get inside and thaw out properly, even though Alex's car was warm enough. The heat she felt inside being near to him made her feel warmer with delight.

"Like I said, it's no trouble at all. I'm glad I was there at the right time."

So was she.

The snow fell harder and the wind swirled snow around reducing the visibility. She was so glad to be with Alex in his truck on the way to his cabin.

Just then she noticed a concerned expression swept across Alex's handsome face as he looked out the windshield.

Something was wrong.

Chapter 4 - Lilly

Lilly noticed Alex's narrowed gaze as he tried to see through the windshield with the decreased visibility outside. He sped up his windshield wipers.

"Oh, no," he said, turning his truck towards a cabin. Was that *his* cabin?

"I'm sorry, Lilly," he said, getting out of the truck after he parked. "I'll just be a second. Looks like my neighbor's in trouble."

"Your neighbor? Oh, of course. Let's help him. Can I come?"

"Sure. And it's her," he corrected Lilly, gently. "It's Mrs. K."

Alex had a very calm and controlled mannerism in the face of unpredictable conditions. She gathered it was from his military training. She admired that about him. Nothing seemed to alarm him. The wind speed picked up and the snow fell harder, swirling around.

Still, she was ashamed to admit she felt a pang of jealousy for some strange reason when he mentioned his neighbor was female...until he said *Mrs.* K. At least she was a married neighbor. Why was Lilly feeling that way? It wasn't as if Alex was hers. Though, if she were being honest with herself, she'd always fantasized about Alex, from the moment they'd met before. He seemed so unreachable at the time. He was her friend's sexy recluse cousin.

"Oh, Alex, thank goodness. Kitty got outside." The older woman said to Alex when they approached her.

"No problem, Mrs. K. I've got this. You go back inside. You don't want to catch a cold."

The woman who wore an open coat over her night gown turned to face Lilly.

"Hello," Mrs. K said, curiosity in her tone.

"Hi there," Lilly replied.

"Oh, I'm sorry," Alex said. "Lilly this is Mrs. K. Mrs. K. This is Lilly. One of Daphne's friends."

"How nice to meet you," Mrs. K said.

"Nice to meet you too," Lilly replied, pleasantly.

"Alex always takes care of me. Ever since my husband passed away. He's so kind. He chopped wood for me and stocked up my fridge in time before the storm."

"He did?" Lilly said, feeling warm inside. Her heart melted. Alex was hot. He rocked a sexy body covered in tattoos, yet here he was, a big teddy bear with a heart of gold who took care of his elderly neighbors. If that wasn't noble and honorable, she didn't know what was.

She'd never met a guy like that before. Ever. "That's so sweet of him," Lilly said. She really meant it. She thought she couldn't be more attracted to Alex but she was now.

"Hey, listen, Alex is right, you should be getting back inside. It's freezing out here." She helped the older woman inside to her cabin.

Later, Alex brought her cat back inside and checked to make sure all the doors and windows were shut tight, including Mrs. K's back door. He closed an open window. He gave the place a once over to make sure everything was safe.

"Remember, to call me if you need anything Mrs. K. Anytime. My phone number's right there on the fridge."

"You are so kind, Alex. Thank you. You two are so sweet, taking care of me. Making sure I'm all right. I do appreciate it. I'll be fine now. I've got everything I need."

"Are you sure?"

"Oh, yes. Kitty is here with me." Mrs. K hugged her cat to her chest.

They stayed for a while to make sure she was all right before heading back on the road. Not before making Mrs. K a cup of tea and making sure she was snug by the fireplace with her book. It melted her heart. She reminded Lilly of her own grandmother before she passed.

"My cabin's not far from Mrs. K, so I'll be checking up on her again later," Alex said, later when they got back into his truck. "Looks like it's going to be quite a storm," he added.

"Yes, it does," Lilly agreed, looking out at the menacing weather. "That was so nice what you did back there with Mrs. K," Lilly added.

"It was nothing. She's a sweet lady. I just like to make sure she's all right. That was nice of what *you* did to get her settled in with her book. You're quite a caregiver." He smiled.

"You should talk. She's lucky to have a neighbor like you."

It didn't take long to get to Alex's cabin.

"Nice," she said, after he opened the door and let her inside his spacious cozy log cabin. She also appreciated him getting out of his truck and going to the passenger side to open her door for her and helping her out. Chivalry was so nice to see around there.

He was a perfect gentleman.

"What would you like? I can make you some hot chocolate to get you warm inside. Dinner won't take long. Got some chicken I can grill with potatoes."

"You're so sweet. Can I help you?"

"You're a guest in my home. I want to take care of you and make sure you're all right. You've had a rough day," he said.

An hour later, the cabin was filled with the aroma of delicious grilled chicken. Alex really knew his way around the kitchen.

The scrumptious taste melted on her tongue.

"So what happened at the retreat?" Alex asked her, later after dinner. He seemed genuinely interested in hearing what she had to say.

"Well, it was a winter company trip with a new client. I worked at an ad agency."

"With your ex?" His brows furrowed.

"Not at first. He worked in another division. He transferred later to my department and became manager. His family are friends with the owners. I didn't know this before."

"I see," he said, a look of genuine interest and concern spread over his sexy facial features. He was so strikingly good looking, it was difficult to concentrate around him. She'd never met a guy this hot before. And man, was he making her feel hot inside.

Desire for him swept inside her but she had to be cool about this. He was her friend's cousin and she wasn't really that experienced. She'd only just had the one boyfriend. Not to mention Alex probably had way more experience than she did.

Lilly tried to shift her focus back on the conversation instead of Alex's strong muscular arms with all those beautiful tattoos, or his shapely lips, his gorgeous blue eyes.

"Anyway, I don't want to bore you," she said, swallowing hard, hoping he wouldn't notice how flushed she was.

"You're not boring me at all. I want to hear about what happened to you. You need to get it off your chest."

"Thanks," she said, melting inside. Was this mountain man for real? He was probably the first guy who ever cared about taking the time to listen to what she had to say. Bonus points for him in her mental notebook.

Okay, Lilly, focus.

It was hard to not focus on Alex's strong muscular arms with the decorative tattoos adorning his smooth skin. His gorgeous face with strong chiseled features and sexy eyes. Man, his eyes were sensuous.

It had been over two years since she'd dated or been close with a man like this. Her ex was her first real boyfriend and after breaking up with him—she hadn't felt this close to a man before. She hadn't had the desire to date again. Until tonight. Until this mountain man rescued her from danger.

"Well," she continued. "Long story short, my ex had been up to his shenanigans again and trying to make things difficult for me. He wanted to get me fired. That's why he kept having meetings and excluding me from the email list or telling me the meeting time would be one hour later than the actual meeting and then accusing me of being late—in front of everyone."

"The guy's an asshole. He can't get away with that." Alex's fury flared. "Why was he being a jerk? I can't imagine anyone treating a beautiful woman like you the way he did."

"Thanks," she said, feeling Alex's sincerity and appreciating him taking her side. Everyone else at the company seemed to feel as if her ex was justified in bullying her. "You see, it's strange but his grandfather left this peculiar will saying that he had to be married by thirty. So he proposed to me. His sweet widowed grandmother approved of me. Anyway, I broke it off when I found out he was cheating on me and so he got angry and said I cost him his inheritance."

"Really now? Looks like he did that to himself."

"You could say that. I guess he wants someone to blame. So that's why he tried to sabotage me."

"If I get my hands on that guy…" Alex pinched his lips together into a thin line.

"It's okay. I never wanted to stay at that job anyway. It was getting way too toxic for me."

"They don't deserve you. But you can't let them get away with this."

"I'll think about that later. I just wished the work break up didn't happen out here. I really wanted to have my own ad agency one day and this new client who owns the mountain winter retreat was one of my favorites. They loved my ideas, even though my ex took the credit for it. I wish I could work with them on my own. We seemed to connect during our initial meeting. Anyway, my ex sabotaged that."

She noticed Alex's eyes narrowed with disgust at what her ex had done.

"Oh, really now?" he said.

"Unfortunately. Anyway, they hadn't signed the contract yet with my ex's agency so I'm not sure what's going to happen now."

"What's the name of the mountain retreat company?"

She told him and he thought for a moment.

"Anyway, it's over and done with. I'll pick myself up and carry on." She told him about her brother's care.

"That's very noble of you, Lilly. You are an earth angel."

"My brother's the earth angel, but thank you for your kind words," she said, softly.

"I want to help you," he said.

"But you've already done so much for me, saving my life." Heat climbed to her cheeks. "I'll figure it out, don't worry. It's not your fault my ex did what he did."

"I can't believe he left you out here in the freezing cold knowing there's a storm brewing."

"That's my ex for you. I don't want to talk about him anymore. That's the past. It might have just happened but it's still the past and right now, I have to figure out how to get back into town."

She heard the wind howling outside the hard pellets of snow pounding on the window of the cabin, knowing deep down, it's unlikely to happen tonight.

The warm glow of the fireplace illuminated Alex's disarmingly handsome features. He looked like a GQ model.

"Would you like something else?"

Just you, she thought.

Why was her body so attracted to this guy? She'd been attracted to him from the first time she met him at the fundraising barbecue.

But he was her friend's cousin. Daphne didn't like her friends dating members of her family. And she couldn't blame her.

"No, thank you. I hate putting you out like this."

"You're not putting me out. It's not every day, a beautiful woman like yourself stops by."

"That's surprising," she said, then bit down on her lower lip. She hoped it didn't come out all wrong. "I mean, you're so…stunning," she said.

Why did she say what was on her mind? It had been two years since she last dated. Maybe it was beginning to get to her. This was so unlike her. She'd always been shy or timid around guys. Her breakup with her ex didn't help much.

"You're a good person, Alex. And a great listener."

Was that rouge on his cheeks? He looked away for a moment.

"Thanks."

"Hey, it's no problem." She paused for a moment then asked, "So what about you? What made you decide to move to the mountains? I'd like to know more about you. We didn't really get a chance to get acquainted last year."

Chapter 5 - Alex

This gorgeous woman wants to know more about me.

Alex couldn't help but feel warm inside at the thought as he and Lilly sat in front of the fireplace on his couch as the snow fell harder and the wind howled outside.

Most women didn't get him and didn't approach him. He thought he always gave off that keep-away-from-me vibe since his breakup—and come to think of it, whenever he was in a relationship. He was a one woman man but he didn't express himself much. Since he moved to the mountains, he was determined to stay single—at least for now.

But how much should he tell Lilly about himself?

He didn't want to scare her away.

Truth was, he had been in a long term relationship. The first real one but it turned out to be a sham.

This rich socialite just wanted to rebel against her folks. When he was with a woman, he was with only her. But it looked as if his ex didn't see things the same way.

After they'd broken up, he didn't trust another woman. His ex certainly didn't care about learning more about him. Everything was materialism for her. That and Instagram images.

So, yeah, his ex had been using him. The whole bad boy image was what attracted her to him. She liked the image of looking as if she were in a relationship with a bad boy.

And he was.

But he would *never* do anything to break a woman's heart. Ever.

He was sincere that way.

"There isn't much to tell," he said, gently.

"Oh, come on," she said, snuggling up to him.

His cock jumped as she hugged his arm.

Man, he was so attracted to her. He wanted to be with her ever since that day he met her at the fundraiser.

He found himself hugging her back.

He felt so comfortable around her. As if they belonged together.

Alex finally gave her a brief rundown of what had happened. Her lips formed a perfect O.

"That's awful, Alex. I'm so sorry you went through that. Your ex didn't deserve you. You are such an honorable guy. I wish all guys were like you. The world would be a better place."

Did she really just say that?

He couldn't believe it. "That's quite a compliment." He didn't know what else to say. He wasn't used to getting nice compliments like that. From anyone.

"It's true."

The scent of her floral perfume turned him on. There was something sweet about her energy—about this gorgeous woman with curves in all the right places.

He wanted to protect her, to comfort her, to be with her.

His cock was hard now. That didn't take long when she was near him. Arousal surged through his body. He wanted her right now, right here.

They cuddled as the storm raged on outside. Much like the storm of his torn feelings inside.

What was he doing? Lilly was his cousin's friend. Daphne didn't like members of her family dating her friends.

Trapped on the mountains during a whiteout with a gorgeous woman.

A woman he'd been attracted to and thought about since last year when he was a single man. But could he tell her that?

Would she freak out? But then again, honesty was good, wasn't it?

He never did get this relationship thing. Or social cues. If he had he would have known his ex was all about image rather than substance.

Just then, Lilly pressed her lips to his arm. "Thank you so much for saving my life out there," she cooed, in a hoarse whisper.

He turned to face her beautiful face and leaned down to her. She then placed her lips on his. He groaned with pleasure. Man, her lips felt soft and tasted sweet as they kissed.

As if they'd been waiting for this moment since they first met.

Chapter 6 - Lilly

Heat and desire coursed through Lilly's veins as she and Alex French kissed on the couch in front of the fireplace as the blizzard raged on outside. Butterflies exploded in her belly. Oh, she loved his sensuous touch.

A cozy romantic feeling swept through the air around them. This felt so right. So amazing. This hot mountain man's lips were so soft and sensational. Her body tingled from head to toe at his touch; his strong, warm hands caressing her body.

Lilly moaned with delight.

"You're so beautiful, Lilly," Alex breathed between sweet kisses to the sensitive side of her neck. She loved the feel of his lips on her skin.

He then slid his hands further down. He pulled away for a moment surveying her body, admiration in his eyes. "You have the most beautiful curves I've ever seen," he smiled.

"Thank you. I don't hear that all the time. Actually, never…"

He grinned. "Well, you deserve to be told that, beautiful."

She leaned into him again and hugged him, her arms around the top of his shoulders. "I want you now," she whispered.

"You comfortable here?"

"In your arms, yes."

His lips curved into a sweet grin. "I have condoms."

"Good," she whispered, seductively.

He then pressed his lips down her arms and romantically circled his fingers around her skin as she quivered with delight. That felt so good.

He really knew how to arouse her, to turn her on. He then slid off her top and then undid her lacey bra freeing her breasts. Her pink nipples were hard like pebbles. He groaned with approval. And leaned down to kiss her breasts. Then he slid his tongue down one breast and covered her nipple with his soft lips. His moist tongue against her nipple caused her sex to pulse hard. He then did this teasing thing with his tongue, stroking her nipple gently while his other hand circled and played with her other nipple. His tongue then flicked on one nipple.

"Oh, god, that feels good," she cried out in pleasure.

He moved slowly down and slid off her panties and she was naked on the soft comfy couch; the log cabin had a romantic orange glow in the dark from the fire in the fireplace. Everything was so calm there, so romantic. She craved being alone with Alex in the mountains. Just the two of them while flurries of snow hit the window panes of the cabin. The heat of passion keeping them warm inside.

He then slid his fingers between her folds, playing with her now wet pussy.

"You like that, baby," he groaned.

She dug her fingers into his strong muscular back. "Yes, oh, Alex, that feels…so…good," her voice trailed off, as she breathed hard and heavy.

"Fuck, you feel so good. I want you to come for me baby," he groaned into her neck as he pressed kisses to her skin.

"Yes," she breathed hard and fast.

He stroked her, teasing the engorged folds while two of his fingers thrust seductively inside her tightness, back and forth, soft then hard. She moaned with pleasure as he then sucked on her nipples one at a time, wishing his hard erection was inside her.

She soon came hard and fast, waves of orgasmic pleasure washed over her as she convulsed in his embrace. He grinned with approval. "God, you're so amazing, Lilly."

She leaned into him and brushed her lips passionately against his. She then slid her hand down to his pants, feeling the hard erection beneath.

"I want you now," she breathed.

"Beg," he said, passionately. "I want you to beg for it, baby."

"Please, I want you, Alex. I need you now," she moaned as they continued to make out.

No one had ever made her come like that before and his hard dick wasn't even inside her yet. She still felt the feel of his warm fingers inside her.

Soon, Alex had slid off his clothes.

"God, you're so fit." Admiration filled her eyes as she admired his ripped muscles on his tattooed skin. He was like a perfect sculpture. So muscular and firm in all the right places. Broad shoulders and lean waist. An impressive V shape of his muscular thighs.

When he slid off his boxers, her eyes widened with delight.

"You're so huge," she said.

"It's all for you, baby," he groaned in a low seductive voice.

Soon, he opened the condom packet and then rolled the condom over his long hard shaft. She stroked his hardness and enjoyed the low groans of pleasure coming from his lips.

"I want to come inside you," he breathed, hoarsely.

She then stopped as he positioned himself over her, kissing her neck and then her lips, whispering how much he adored her and treasured her.

He positioned his cock at the entrance to her small opening as he lovingly gazed into her eyes. His sexy blue eyes penetrating hers. Then, he slowly moved his thick erection inside her small pussy, moving slow at first back and forth as she arched her back with pleasure, tightening around his impressive shaft, breathing hard.

He then moved his hips in rhythmic motion as he thrust in and out of her, back and forth, slowly then faster. Oh, this felt so good. Waves of pleasure swept through her body.

Soon, he was thrusting inside her deeper and harder as she tightened around him again, enjoying the full sensation as he hit all the right spots inside her sensitive area.

She loved the feel of his huge cock inside her as he filled her, moving inside her while deep groans sounded from his lips. Their warm bodies pressed up against each other as he made love to her, fucking her hard and fast until she came with another wave of orgasmic release, her body jerking with pleasure overload. Alex came hard and fast soon after and they soon collapsed into each other's arms and hugged, cuddling in front of the fireplace.

"God, you're so amazing, Lilly. You are the most gorgeous woman I've ever been with."

"You're amazing too, Alex."

They kissed and cuddled, sated with pleasure and comfort.

This was certainly the most memorable way to be stranded in the middle of a blizzard with a hot mountain man and enough heat between them to melt the snow outside. The wind howled outside as she lay in Alex's warmth, his muscular body protectively hugging her.

But she wanted more of Alex. She really didn't want this moment to ever end. She wanted to see Alex again after this. One night would never be enough.

***

The following morning, Lilly woke up with a wide smile on her face. She couldn't remember when she last woke up that way. The other side of the bed was warm where Alex had laid last night, after they'd made love a few more times. This sinfully gorgeous mountain man had so much stamina. It amazed her.

He was hot in bed. Sexy and wonderful in every way.

But could this work?

What would happen now?

The aroma of bacon and eggs wafted to her nostrils. Was Alex in the kitchen making breakfast?

Just then the bedroom door opened and Alex walked into the room with a tray of breakfast along with a vase and a flower inside.

"Oh my goodness. I feel as if I'm in a hotel or resort."

"Morning, beautiful," he said and kissed her.

"Good morning, handsome," she grinned. "Thank you," she said as he handed her the breakfast tray, placing it over her legs as she sat up on the bed.

"Hey, it's no problem at all."

"Alex, I had a wonderful time with you last night," she said.

"I did too," he said, looking into her eyes with admiration. "I've never met anyone as beautiful as you Lilly, inside and out."

"Aww, Alex."

"It's true. And I know this might be awkward being that you're the friend of my cousin, but I want us to see more of each other."

"So would I. I would love to."

"I'm sure Daphne will be okay with it. But even so, I've never felt this way about anyone before. I've been admiring you from afar since last year and never knew if we'd meet up again."

"I guess fate had a hand in that," she said.

He bit down on his lower lip before saying. "I hope you don't mind but I made a call early this morning to one of the guys I served with."

"Oh," she said, curious.

"He happens to own the mountain retreat company that your former ad agency is courting."

"What?" Lilly's eyes widened in surprise.

"Let's just say we're close and he owes me one. He would love to meet with you if you're still interested owning your own ad agency and acquiring new clients."

"Oh, my god! Are you serious!" This would be her dream! She'd always wanted to have her own ad agency and if the mountain retreat company was her first client, that would be all she needed with that lucrative contract. In fact, she wouldn't need any other clients right now—and she could cover her brother's medical expenses for a long time.

"Yes, I'm very serious when it comes to someone I care deeply about." He looked deeply into her eyes, and her heart turned over with joy in her chest. "I know we haven't known each other for long. But I can tell a lot about a person."

She wrapped her arms around him. "Thank you, Alex."

"Hey, it's nothing."

"Yes it is. You saved my life and now, my career." She didn't think her ex would be happy about that but he'd put himself in that situation.

"Nothing's too good for you, Lilly." His voice was deep, reassuring, low and sexy.

They both glanced out the window at the blizzard outside. The weather still wasn't letting up.

"I never believed in love at first sight or kismet before I met you," he said.

She smiled, warmly.

"I'd love to spend more time with you and see where it goes," he added.

She hugged him tightly and pressed her lips to his, giving him a warm kiss. "I'm happy to see where this goes too. I have a good feeling about this."

Being stranded in the blizzard with Alex, the wonderfully caring and stunningly gorgeous mountain man, was the best thing that's happened to Lilly in a long while.

And she would love to spend forever with him.

Books by Ann Ric

Mountain Men of Charming Falls

Rescued by the Mountain Man (Evie & Jake)
Claimed by the Mountain Man (Candi & Erik)
Stranded with the Mountain Man (Lilly & Alex)
Christmas with the Mountain Man (Harmony & Chase)

Magic Protector Reverse Harem Trilogy

Magic Protector – A Steamy Paranormal Reverse Harem Romance (Book 1)
Magic Bound – A Steamy Paranormal Reverse Harem Romance (Book 2)
Magic Promise – A Steamy Paranormal Reverse Harem Romance (Book 3)

Mountain Men of Charming Falls

"Love makes the world go 'round"

Welcome to ***Mountain Men of Charming Falls***, the spicy instalove series based on a picturesque small mountain town by a lake that brings you closer to nature. A tranquil scenic escape from the busy city where residents in the cozy close-knit community look out for each other. Let the cool mountain breeze, clear night skies, beautiful romantic sunsets, and the fresh pine scents that fill the air bring you serene relaxation. Known for its camping sites, rustic cabin retreats, hiking trails, ski slopes, and yes, semi-recluse hot and sexy ex-military mountain men who live by the honor code: respect, loyalty, selfless service, integrity and courage in everything they do. Charming Falls is the perfect place to fall in love.

Rescued by the Mountain Man (Mountain Men of Charming Falls Book 1)

Rescued by the Mountain Man is a sweet & steamy short instalove romance novella featuring a gorgeous ex-military mountain man and a curvy woman.

Evie is a wedding planner-turned-jilted bride. She became a viral meme when she ran out of the chapel on her wedding day in tears. Why did she live-stream her wedding? Who was she to have it streamed? It wasn't like she was marrying a prince. She'd walked out of her wedding to her now ex-groom when a surprise guest showed up...

His wife!

Yep, that's right. She didn't know her now ex-groom was already married. So much for happily ever after. Humiliated and broken-hearted, she decides to go to a quaint small town where no one knows her; into the woods of the mountain town of Charming Falls to escape. To vanish. To disappear. Until she gets confronted by a bear...

Ex-military soldier and volunteer builder, Jake, wants to escape his past and live alone. Being a recluse in Charming Falls works for him…until a beautiful curvy woman shows up in distress. Will she be the one to break the protective barrier over his heart?

Claimed by the Mountain Man (Mountain Men of Charming Falls Book 2)

A sweet, grumpy ex-military mountain man and a shy, curvy wedding floral arranger. An undeniable chemistry. Can love bring them together?

When Candi, a talented floral designer who makes floral arrangements for lonely patients or deserving brides on a budget, finds herself lost on the mountains without cell phone service on her way to her friend's wedding, she knows she's in trouble…

Until she's rescued by a gorgeous mountain man with biceps of steel and a sweet, grumpy demeanor. Should she trust her heart around this handsome recluse?

Stranded with the Mountain Man (Mountain Men of Charming Falls Book 3)

After her boss, who is also her ex, leaves her at the company's camping trip site, Lilly finds herself stranded in the middle of a brewing storm...

Until she's rescued by a gorgeous, grumpy ex-military mountain man with the most breathtaking physique and stunning features she's ever seen. She's supposed to be on a break from dating, so why is she falling for this hero?

Christmas with the Mountain Man Mountain Men of Charming Falls Book 4)

After her now-ex broke off with her last Christmas, Harmony decided to never marry or celebrate the holidays...but her godmother had other plans. Harmony finds herself in Charming Falls to put up the Christmas tree in her godmother's *Happily Ever After* log cabin while she's away. But she soon runs into unexpected trouble in the form of a strikingly gorgeous mountain man.

Ex-military mountain man Chase wasn't looking for love, until love came to his door...his mother's friend asked him to put up the Christmas tree in her log cabin. But he wasn't expecting an intruder; a beautiful curvy woman...

*"Think of the things that make you happy,
not the things that make you sad..."*

-    Robert E. Farley

Coming soon...

More sizzling short romance novellas in the Mountain Men of Charming Falls series by Ann Ric

ABOUT THE AUTHOR

Ann Ric enjoys writing steamy paranormal romance novels and sizzling hot contemporary romance short stories with a happily ever after. She loves to read romance novels featuring strong characters and breathtaking worlds. You can reach her by email at heartandsoulbooks7@gmail.com

Milton Keynes UK
Ingram Content Group UK Ltd.
UKHW041822131124
451149UK00001B/18

9 798227 068163